EDITED & COMPILATION – DR MEETA NIHALANI DMS JNVU
JODHPUR

I0530505

Celebrating & Converging Life Through Positivity

A Journey to Discover Secrets of Life

Author - Mr. Shyam Dewani Senior Advocate Nagpur & Bombay High Court
Dewani Associates

23/3/2020

"This book celebrates the memories and sentiments of life, designed to live in a positive way. Life is a beautiful journey to build trust and positive ethics of respecting each other. The beauty of life, lies in celebrating the moments of joy for creating success through commitment and hard work"- Pooja Nihalani.

Contents

Preface

Converging life is the new way of creating culture to imbibe and connect with the evolving world. The ideas and thoughtscan help people to grow in an empowered way, by creating social trust and happiness. The ethics and values of life can be shaped by the beautifulparticipation of people, to read and connect for converging to increase their relations and business. These communities and forums have become important for me to design the society and family of my dreams.

The positivethoughts can be a force of change to create moral values of tolerancefor bondingpeople through education. These bits of information can move in a faster and easy wayto build quality life for people, by the creative use of resources to develop activities.

Life, designed with goodness of sharing, with everybody can create strength of believingin the power of social bonding. The warmness of togetherness can only be celebrated with the positive wishes and concernfor each other in the society. The strength of being, connected in family and relatives, candesign the present and future fabric of life. Life is series of beautiful grains of actions, duties andethics with commitment and loyalty to build a huge system of working and growing together. As an individual, weneed respect and dignity to build faith and trust in our work, family and professional life.

Acknowledgement

This is a beautiful expression of my thoughts, to connect with all the members, who are associated with me, in my professional and personal life. The inspiration from my parentsMr. Dayaram Dewami & Mrs Sushila Dewani, has given me the strength to shape this bookwith values and ethics of respecting and loving people.

I thank my wife Mrs.Rajeshree Dewani for being an empowered pillar of my life. She has been a constant source of positivity fordesigningmy dreams. My son Mr. Sahil Dewani has been silentlysupporting and connecting to allmy professional effortsfor building the intellectual wealth. The love and affection of my daughter Pooja has made the colors of life more intense and deep. MyGurus gave me the talent and abilities to contribute to society. They have created my life and given me a sense of fulfillment to grow academically.

I am connected to my teammates of professional life, who have supported and inspired to design, this beautiful journey of my life. My relationships of professional life are the most precious assets of my work life.

CHAPTER 1

RELATIONSHIPS AND PURPOSE OF LIFE

Introduction

The value of life is decided by the quality of relationships,surrounding our existence. Relationships are the reflection of our inner soul and personality. The basic ability to connect with people, in a respectful way, can help us to define the ethics and avenues of relationships. I cherish to have all these precious relationships to build an innate impact and fulfillment in my life. The way, we connect with people, can help us to find the solutions of all problems of our life. The intensity of relationships can give us the power to define ourselves through the teams and families to work and grow in an expressive way. The positive vibes of relationshipscan give us the fulfillment and happiness for being loved and protected. The precious moments ofjoy and togetherness can only be celebrated through the warmness of possessing quality relationships.

Purpose of life

Our prime purpose in this life is to help others & if we can't help them, at least don't hurt them.Our work is going to fill a large part of our life, & the only way to be truly satisfied is to do, what we believe is great work & the only way to do great work is to love, what we do. Sometimes our heart needs, more time to accept, what our mind already knows. Our circumstances have little to do with our success or failure.Non-achievers blame the circumstances for their failure. Winners rise above all of their adverse circumstances & achieve their goal. While the unsuccessful people concentrate on the blank walls that stare at them.

The winners always try to get under it, over it, around it or through it.

- Don't be a fence sitter or loser
- Be a winner always
- Live a better life by controlling your stress
- Control your stress by not worrying about things that you can't change.

Live the Life of Dreams

Be brave enough to live the life of dreams, according to the vision& purpose, instead of the expectations & opinions of others.If people have a strong purpose in life, they   don't have to be pushed. Their passion will drive them there.Fear has two meanings: 'forget everything and run' or 'face everything and rise.' Once people become fearless, life becomes limitless. When the roots are deep, there is no reason to fear the wind. Never give up, & be confident. There may be tough times, but the difficulties which people face will make them more determined to achieve their objectives and to win against all the odds.It's easier to go down a hill than up it but the view is much better at the top.

Summary

Relationships need the touch of care and love to build the intensity of warmness. The connections can design the destiny of people because we live in groups and the sharing helps us to create our goal. The definition ofrelationships, very abstract but still these are themost vital part of our life. The quality of relationships can change the meaning of life for people. They help them to grow with confidence and faith. The closeness of people, can also build the trust of facing everything with courage and faith. The motivation to live can only be designed by having good relationships in forms of friends and family .Life touched with the faith and love of intense relationships can help any individual to achieve his goal.

CHAPTER 2

WORK AND HABITS

Introduction

The destiny of life isdefined by the kind of habits; people have, for their work life. The modern culture of work life balance has changed to blending life with work. The reflection of human personality is imbibed with the impact and values of his work life. The professionalism of human life designs the ego, confidence and self-respect of any individual. The progress and growth of life revolves, around the ethics and activities of working with positive habits of having commitment and faith in individual values. The belief of doing good workcan bring results for organization and family. This can help the social systems to be more empowered, where values can create positive governance.

Designing Destiny

Eliminate today's troubles and problems, by finding solutions, & then energy on implementing those solutions. Live without pretending, love without depending, listen without defending, and speak without offending. Destiny will never gift success.It can lend opportunities& possibilities.It is for people to convert them in success.There are two things in this world which we cannot estimate the value. They are peace & satisfaction.Those who earn these two things will definitely enjoy endless happiness. In order to live in peace, try to not depend on anyone & at the same time try to help others, not to, depend on anyone. Help them to become independent, free & responsible for their lives.

Sometimes, we have to make a big mistake to figure out, how to make things right! .Mistakes are painful, but they're the only way to find out the reality.So, we should never be too worried about the mistakes but learn from the experience gained& be determined to, not to, repeat them.A failure is not always a mistake; it may simply be the best one can do under the circumstances. The real mistake is to stop trying. We should stay true to you, yet always be open to learn. Work hard, & never give up on dreams, even when nobody else believes, they can come true. These are not clichés but real tools needed. No matter, whatpeople do in life, stay focused on path.Don't wait for doing good work to make place in the memories of people. Do it now, believing there is no tomorrow.

Worries are like moon, one day it will increase, One day it will decrease, other day it may not be seen...so don't worry for anything. The worries won't change situations, not it will improve our health.

Power of Habits

Three power habits to elevate our life.

1. Encourage instead of criticizing
2. Understand instead of judging.
3. Initiate instead of waiting.

Sticking to good habits can be hard work, & mistakes are part of the process.Don't declare failure simply because you messed up or because you're having trouble reaching your goals. Instead, use your mistakes as opportunities to grow stronger & become better.

The difference between a successful person & others is not a lack of strength, not a lack of knowledge, but rather a lack of will.If somebody gives his trust to a person, who does not deserve it,he actuallygives the power to destroy him. Trust' is a small word; takes a second to read it, a minute to think about it, a day to understand it, but to prove it, an entire life.Problems tend to growl at us, like cowardly barking dogs.If we face them & challenge them, they back away. If we run from them, they run after us, snapping our heels.There's no use talking about the problem, unless we talk about the solution because, we cannot solve our problems with the same level of thinking that created them.

Summary

The work life of any individual can be designed by his faith in work. Theconnections of people to their work habits can make them successful or unsuccessful. People tend to create money, wealth andrespect, through their communication with work. Work habits, help people to create their identity and credibility in the society. The individuals need to have positive orientation towards their work. The challenge of life is to accept work with dignity and face the problems and issues, with confidence and positive faith. There is always a way for people, who have will to work with deep desires to excel and grow.

CHAPTER 3

POWER OF POSITIVE VALUES

Introduction

The power of positive values can create wonders with the human life. If people have faith and trust with the power to believe andconnect with the spiritualpowers of god, then they can have success in life. The positive power of values can help them to grow with empowerment. People canachieve anything, if they are able to believe and live in positive social systems. Thepositivevalues can be generated if people are educated and believe in the region of humanity which is above cast and creed. The connections can create wariness and also help to solve their problems. Thepositivefaith of having trust canssocieties with high social capital which can build the spiritual wealth any country. .

Acceptance with Strength of Believing

A positive thinker would say, I will decide my fate & my own destiny. Everyone appears to be courageous until bad weathers arrive, & then we know the true leaders. Great occasions do not make heroes or cowards; they simply unveil them to the eyes of men. Silently & perceptibly, as we wake or sleep. We grow strong or weak; & last some crisis shows what we have become. A coward hides behind freedom. A brave person stands in front of freedom & defends it for others

Every great dream begins with a dreamer. People always have strength, patience, and passion to reach for stars to change the world.The key to everything is patience. The key to realizing a dream is to focus not on success but significance, and then even the small steps & little victories along your path will take on greater meaning.Life is too precious to stress yourself out by worrying about everything. Relax, have fun, & enjoy the learning process.

Many times what we perceive as an error or failure is actually a gift & eventually we find that lessons learned from that discouraging experience prove to be of great worth.Mistakes have the power to turn people into something better, than they werebefore. We are products of our past, but we don't have to be prisoners.If somebody offers an amazing opportunity but if person is are not sure he can do it, say yes – then learn how to do it later; because opportunities are like sunrises, if people wait too long, they miss them.If people miss an opportunity, they should not cloud eyes, with tears but keep vision clear, so that they will not miss the next one.Acceptance is not a state of passivity or inaction. We can't change the world, right wrongs, or replace evil with good.

Acceptance and Faith

Acceptance is, in fact, the first step to successful action.If people don't fully accept a situation precisely the way it is, they will have difficulty changing it. Moreover, if they don't fully accept the situation, they will never really know, if the situation should be changed.Life is a series of natural & spontaneous changes. Don't resist them; that only creates sorrow. Let reality be reality.Let things flow naturally forward in whatever way they like.Never give up, & be confident. There may be tough times, but the difficulties which people face, will make them more determined to achieve their objectives& to win against all the odds.

If we fall behind, run faster. It does not matter how slowly we go, as long as we do not stop. Never give up, never surrender, & rise up against the odds.Something, that is very special today, might not be special tomorrow, but to hold it, to grasp it, to keep it, to make it special, to elevate it from the ordinary, that's when we open up the champagne. To make it sparkle. Embrace each challenge in life as an opportunity for self-transformation.

Summary

The power of positive values can go a long way to design the beauty of life. We need to thank god for all the blessings and happiness, bestowed on us. The power of feeling the possessionof intangiblewealth can help us to live healthy life, where there is less frustration, jealousy and hatred for each other. The simplicity of life can be filled with love and affection. People should not indulge in self-hatred and depression. Acceptance of human power can be the greatest blessing for society. People need to think and build the power of getting the things done through cooperation and support, which can create a network.

CHAPTER 4

SIMPLICITY AND HUMILITY

Introduction

The simplicity and humility can open infinite doors of growth for any human personality. People can get respect, in society, if they are able to connect with each other with simplicity and humility. The actualself-esteem ofpeople is reflectedthrough humility towards others in society. People need acceptance, so they can connect with each other. The value of connections, gives the power of doing work with confidence and faith. The success of any organization depends on the humility of people to support and communicate with teammembers, with the utmost humility. The decisions can also be taken in a positive way, if people are ready to communicate with humility. The simplicity of thoughts can help in better connections to grow with positive ethics of trust and faith. Humility helps in relatingwith real worth, of any individual. People with humility, can learn more and grow with power of simplicity. The pride and self-faithcan be reflected, if people have humility and simplicity to accept, as they are, with their differences of cultures and values.

Empowering Oneself

Simplicity &humility are traits which are highly empowering. Instead of grabbing attention, we'd try to highlight the work & performance of others.There is always a tendency on the part of some people to take all the credit, even when it is not due to them & pass on the blame to others.

It is cheap to blow one's own trumpet or boast about oneself. Don't do what is best for oneself but for the good for everyone connected. Never be self-centered. Have an open mind & work towards the overall wellbeing& progress of everyone concerned.Beliefs don't make a better person but the behaviorcreates the value of an individual. There is no greater fear than the fear of uncertainty because the unknown is something that can't be looked in the face, challenged, overcome. We all have challenges. We have to face them, embrace them, defy them, & conquer them & not to run away from them.Whatever the mind can conceive & believe, it can achieve. The mind is everything. What people think, they become, □what they feel attract. what they imagine, they create.□□□□□□□□□□□□

Mind precedes all mental states. Mind is the chief. If with a pure mind a person speaks or acts, happiness follows him,like his never-departing shadow.Inside each of us, there is the seed of both good and evil.It's a constant struggle, as to which one will win & one cannot exist without the other.Keep away from people, who try to belittle ambitions. Small people always do that, but the really great can make a person great.

Everyone seems to have a clear idea of how other people, should lead their lives, but none about his or her own. Reach goals and live life before life leaves. Life is like an ocean, with waves that will rise &fall. Learn to stand firm with faith that the waves are there to show the strength - not to wash away! If people want to conquer the anxiety of life, live in the moment, live in the breath.Most mistakes happen by situations, not by intention.So, always try to know the reason behind every mistake of our loved ones. That is the way to value a relation.Good people make mistakes & don't hurt others - then they learn from their mistakes & try not to make them again. Let today be the day. Finally release from the imprisonment of past grudges & anger. Simplify life.

Overcoming the Past

Let go off the poisonsof past& live the abundantly beautiful present. Todayhold hands instead of grudges, spread cheer instead of bitterness, build bridges instead of walls, and strengthen bonds instead of prejudices.It is okay to experience painful, sharp pain from time to time. People willneed to become a better pencil. The most important part of a person will always be what's on the inside.People will make mistakes, everyone does, but that's why pencils have erasers. They can always make a change. Lastly, make mark& continue to write, never give up.Sometimes a mistake can end up being the best decision ever made. If people have a dream, don't just sit there. Gather courage to believe that people can succeed & leave no stone unturned to make it a reality. Everything that happens in life is not fixed; it can be changed by a weapon called will power

A sum can be put right: but only by going back till people find the error & working it afresh from that point, never by simply going on or by being at the point of error. Explain anger, don't express it&people will immediately open the door to solutions instead of arguments.Circumstances have little to do with success or failure. Non-achievers blame the circumstances, for their failure.Winners rise above all of their adverse circumstances & achieve their goal.

While the unsuccessful, people concentrate on blank walls that stare at them, the winners always try to get under it, over it, around it or through it.Don't be a fence sitter or loser is a winner always. Fear is the main source of superstition, & one of the main sources of cruelty.to conquer fear is the beginning of wisdom. Be brave & take risks: people need to have faith in themselves.They don't have to have it, all figure out to move forward. Don't stress much about the closed door behind. They can only reach the newly opened door, if people keep moving forward.There is a little difference in people, but that little difference can make a big difference. That little difference is attitude. The bigger difference is whether it is positive or negative.

Summary

The simplicity and humility of life can help people to learn and design goodsthings with their behavior of being humble. People are born, with their value systems, so they need to overcome the fears ofpast and live with dignity. The self-faith can be enhancing, if people have simplicity and humility to live with faith, in intangible values of life. The faith, trust, connections andinterpersonal links can help people to designan m life with fulfillment and flamboyance.

CHAPTER 5

POSITIVE ATTITUDE CAN WORK WONDERS

Introduction

Attitude is a way of living and can build good orientation towards life and situations. Attitudes create the way, for reacting, towards people and situations.Attitudes can create feelings of trust and happiness for creating positive connections to take responsibilities.

The attitude can be designed, by keeping good friends who can support and help for designing warmness and happiness in life. The mind should be filled with positive inputs to control body. The reflection of body throughpositiveimpacts can attract all good work to life. The interest and habit to take responsibility can help to form good groups and teams. The positive attitude in life can be designed by having positive goals and missions, which can go a long way for connecting and growing. People are responsible for their own actions and activities. Learning and reading, can build faith and abilities in life. The present moments can become beautiful, if people can take additional tasks, for designing creative ideas in their own subjects

Positive Attitudes can Overcome Challenges of Life

A positive attitude can work wonders in a person's life, professional career & even in family. A negative attitude, on the contrary, can lead to disastrous consequences on all fronts & ruin relationships.in short, attitude is everything. So, we should always try to wear our positive attitude & make rapid inroads in the path of success.Sometimes it's the smallest decisions that can change our life forever. How to win in life: work hard complainless.

Listen more and try, learn, grow, don't let people to tell that itcan't be done andmake no excuses.

Challenges are what makes life interesting & overcoming them, is what makes life meaningful. To laugh is to risk appearing a fool, to weep is to risk appearing sentimental. To reach out to another, is to risk involvement. To expose feelings, is to risk exposing true self. To place ideas& dreams before a crowd is to risk their loss.to love is, to risk not being loved in return. To hope is to risk ispain. To try is to risk failure; but risks must be taken, because the greatest hazard in life is to risk nothing.

Don't be too timid & squeamish about actions. Life is an experiment. The more experiments, people make it, is better.Every closed door isn't locked & even if it is, people just might have the key! Search within, to unlock a world of possibilities. Step through new doors. The majority of time, there's something fantastic on the other side. Winning is great, sure, but if people are really going to do something in life, the secret is learning how to lose. Nobody goes undefeated all the time. If they can pick up, after a crushing defeat, & go on to win again, they are going to be a champion someday.

Winner is the one, who always dreams according to his condition. But the person,who changes his condition, as per his dreams, is true champion.Because one believes in oneself, one doesn't try to convince others. Because one is content with oneself,one doesn't need others' approval. Because one accepts oneself, the whole world accepts him or her. Ifthey want peace, stop living in the pieces of past. People are as whole,they decide to be. It well takes some work, start with believing in the worth.

Life is a Road for Riding

Life is one big road with lots of signs. So when people are riding through the ruts, don't complicate mind, flee from hate, mischief and jealousy. Don't bury thethoughts; put vision to reality. Wake up & live!Some days are just bad days that are all. We have to experience sadness to know happiness, & remind self that not every day is going to be a good day, that's just the way it is. The happiest people don't have the best of everything; they just make the best of everything they have. Stay positive in every situation. Never stop trying, have faith, don't stop due to failure. If people believe, they can do things, they are already halfway there.Positive thinking isn't about expecting the best to happen every time, but it's always accepting that whatever happens is the best. Prestige comes when, people   feel, they have done something well. But, honor comes when others feel a person has done something well. Always try to help others.

Take good care of reputation because it is the only thing that will live longer. Happiness, true happiness, is an inner quality. It is a state of mind. If themind is at peace, people are happy. If the mind is at peace, but people have nothing else, they can be happy.If they have everything, the world can give - pleasure, possessions, power - but lack peace of mind, can never make them happy. Happiness does not come from doing easy work but from the afterglow of satisfaction that comes after the achievement of a difficult task that demanded our best.

Summary

Life has to be designedwith courageousattitude, where people need combination of positive circumstances, to create options and opportunities of their choice. They need to stabilize their life, with the positive approach. Happiness and satisfaction can be a way of living in an ethical way to connect .The positive way of life; can build the concept of designing confidence to create values of self-love and respect. Positive attitude can also create self-control to indulge in constructive activities for the growth and progress of human life.

CHAPTER 6

CONFIDENCE AND BELIEF IN YOURSELF

Introduction

People gain strength, courage, & confidence by their experience. They need to build confidence to overcome their fear and stress. The confidence of positive faith, can build constructive psychology to connect with good people in society. The personalconfidencecan help in makingprogress towardsgoals that are far bigger. People need to design a life of good mental health to control situations for designing cooperation and support for each other. The destiny of life is the result of series of activities taken by people to grow in a better way. Everyday people add bricks to build connections fordesigning strong relationships of faith and trust. Stronger are the relationships with people, higher is the ability of people to grow in a bonded way.

OvercomingTough Times and Difficulties

Never give up, & be confident in what people have. There may be tough times, but the difficulties, which people face, will, make them more determined to achieve the objectivesand win against all the odds. If people really believe in then they need to do hard work. Take nothing personally & if something blocks one route, find another. Never give up.Stay positive & happy. Work hard & don't give up hope. Be open to criticism &keep learning. Get surroundedby happy, warm & genuine people. The positive thinker sees the invisible, feels the intangible, & achieves the impossible.

Never be bullied into silence. Neverallow to be made a victim. Accept no one's definition of the life, but define to believe in self,& the rest will fall into place. Have faith in the abilities, work hard& there is nothing thatcannot be accomplished.Successful people do what unsuccessful people are not willing to do. Don't wish, it was easier; wish it is better.Success in this life is not final. Failure is not fatal. The only thing that counts is courage to persevere.

Golden rules of

A positive lifestyle -

1. Before assume, learn the facts.

2. Before judge, understand, why.

3. Before hurt someone, feel.

4. Before speak, think.

The assumptions are the windows on the world.Scrub them off, every once in a while, or the light won't come in.Life is beautiful. Life doesn't change. Have a day, a night, a month, & a year. We people change - we can be miserable or we can be happy. It's what makes life.Don't waste time, looking back for what is lost.Move on, for life is not meant to be travelled backwards.

In life, we all may have the followings:

An unspeakable secret

- An irreversible regret
- An unkempt promise
- An unheard promise
- An irreplaceable loss
- An unreachable dream

Still life is about being happy because everything in life can be summed up in four words:"*Life must go on*".

Prescription for a Happy Life

Life gives hundred reasons to cry, show life that person can have a thousand reasons to smile. When there is time, there is no money. And when there is money, there is no time. So, if people, don't want to have regrets in this life, they need to do it, when they have either of them,don't wait for both. Every moment & situation in this life is temporary. When life seems good, rememberand enjoy it to the fullest & when it's not, just remember that it's not going to stay like this forever.Every mistake has its own way to correct self.Every sadness has its reason.Every tear has its own explanation. Every heartbreak has its own history but whatever it is, always remember that at the end of this, we will end up with learning a lesson.

Distance never kills a relation, closeness never builds a relation, it's the caring of one's feelings that builds faith & maintains a relation. So never explain one because real friends don't need it & enemies' won't believe it.Beliefs don't make a better person. Person's behavior does! There's a difference between interest & commitment. When interested in doing something, do it only, when it's convenient. When committed to something, accept, no excuses; only results.

Promises don't make a better person, commitment does. Success means doing the best; we can with what we have. Success is doing, not gettingin trying, not the triumph. Success is a personal standard, reaching for the highest that is in us, becoming all that we can be.Don't get jealous of someone who is ahead; rather take a cue from him to succeed inlife. Success is always between person & mind!Whenever in conflict with someone, there is one factor that can make the difference between damaging relationship & deepening it. That factor is attitude.

Every relationship has cracks.Tear it apart with anger or fill the gaps with forgiveness, the choice is in person's hand. Trust the instincts, go inside, and follow heart, right from the start. Go ahead & stand up for what,they believe in. That is the path to happiness. The biggest obstacle to happiness is undervaluing what person has& overvaluing what others have.If someone decides, they're not going to be happy, it's not the problem. People don't have to spend time and energy, trying to cheer up someone, who has already decided to stay in a bad mood. Believe it or not, people can actually hurt someone, by playing into his self-pity.No matter how painful & difficult decisions   havebeen made in life but if a person can sleep well, at night without guilt, rest assured.

A pessimist sees difficulty in every opportunity; an optimist sees an opportunity in every difficulty. Opportunities are usually disguised as hard work, so most people don't recognize them.We should follow four simple steps of ant philosophy and we will see the difference they make to our lives.

1. Don't quit.

2. Look ahead.

3. Stay positive.

4. And do all you can.

And there is just one more lesson to be learnt from ants. An   ant can carry objects up to 20 times its own weight. Maybe we are like that too. We can carry burdens on our shoulders & manage workloads that are far, far heavier than we would imagine.Think of the little ant. & remember, there is so much stress in life, it'sbecause we focus too much on improving our lifestyle, rather than our 'life'!

People are not obligated to win. They are obligated to keep trying. To do the best, they need to do every day. Ifthey don't see themselves winners, they will never be able to perform as a winner.We are exactly what we think ourselves, to be, let's quit being our own worst enemy, & today be our own best friend

Don't be the person, who needs someone, besomeone's as needed. How far people go in life is a choice. Never let excuses doubt or negativity slow down. Take a chance & become unstoppable.If people are depressed, they are living in the past. If they are anxious, they are living in the future. If people are at peace,they are living in the present. Always be, a part of the solution, not the problem.

Happiness is a Wonderful Gift

Happiness is a wonderful gift. It makes our day bright & cheerful &gives optimism, to do new things in life. So always, try to be happy & make others feel happy. Happiness is a choice. People can choose to be happy. There's going to be stress in life, but it's their choice whether they let it affect or not.Life's under no obligation, to give what they expect. When life is sweet, say thanks & celebrate. And when life is bitter, say thanks & grow.

It doesn't matter, if the glass is half empty or half full. Be thankful to have a glass - & grateful, that there's something in it.Conditions are always good, never bad. We need to know, how to make good use of them. The man who waits for conditions to improve, may have to wait for eternity!People have to get up every morning with determination. If theyare going to go to bed, with satisfaction. Stress is the gap between expectations& reality. More the gap, more the stress. So expect nothing and accept everything.Always have attitude of 'fact-finding', not 'fault finding'. More smiling, less worrying. More compassion, less judgment. More blessed, less stressed. More love, less hate. Live a lifeof dreams. When people start living a lifeof dreams, there will always be obstacles, doubters, mistakes & setbacks along the way.

But with hard work, perseverance & self-belief, there is no limit to what people can achieve. Start by doing what's necessary, then do what's possible & suddenly a person starts doing the impossible.

Great hopes can be realized; most wonderful dreams can come true. That entire people really needcan have. An incredible goodness is operating on people behalf. If they are living a paltry life, resolve to stop it today. Expect great things to happen.Today is not just another day, but another possible chance to achieve, what people couldn't achieve yesterday. So get on feet& chase after success. Every day, we have plenty of opportunities to get angry, stressed or offended. But what people are doing, when they indulgein these negative emotions is giving something outside self-powerover happiness.

Explain anger, don't express it&people will immediately open the door to solutions instead of arguments.Just as we develop our physical muscles through overcoming opposition - such as lifting weights - we develop our character muscles, by overcoming challenges & adversity.Challenges are like trees seen through a running train. As we approach them, they grow bigger, once we pass them, they become smaller.so never be afraid of them.

Sometimes life is hard, so we have to squeeze it, touch it, play with it, & make it soft like dough! Then when, it is soft enough, we can shape it in any way, we want. Keep moving, touching life, as this will keep it smooth & fun! .We all have the power to shape our day & life, so no matter, what is happening in our lives, we can make decision to be happy & enjoy every moment.Many times, what we perceive, as an error or failure is actually a gift. And eventually, we find that lessons learned from that discouraging experience prove to be of great worth.

If people translate every mistake of life into a positive one, theywill never be a prisoner of past but a designer of the future.No relationship is all sunshine, but two people can share one umbrella & survive the storm together. Whenever in conflict with someone, there is one factor that can make the difference between damaging relationship & deepening it. That factor is attitude.Don't let hard times, forget all blessings. When life is sweet, saysthanks & celebrates. When life is bitter say thanks & grows. Sometimes people face difficulties, not because, theyare doing something wrong, but because they are doing something right. It can be stormy sometimes but it can't rain forever.So keep the head up & put all experiences in a box labeled,thankout.Don't let the noise of others' opinions drain out our inner voice. Have the courage to follow heart and intuition.Don't live the same day over & over again & call that a life. Life is about evolving mentally, spiritually, & emotionally. People need to adjust themselves likewater; in any situation & shape but most importantly they need to create their own way to flow.

Time is a sort of river of passing events and current; no sooner, is a thing brought to sight than it is swept byanother. Time is the most elastic element of the world, because it increases the minutes, when we are waiting & decreases the hours when we are enjoying.The most difficult thing is the decision to act, the rest is merely tenacity. The fears are paper tigers. People can do anything, if they decide to do. They can act to change and control life; & the procedure; the process is its own reward.

Everything,in life is a reflection of a choice people have made. If they want a different result, make a different choice. They can't change the past but can ruin the present by worrying over the future.Don't waste too much of time, over regrets for mistakes, take them as just lessons learned & move on. Life would be a lot easier, if they could put feelings& thoughts into actions.Life is too deep for words; so don't try to describe it, just live it. Nothing in life is to be answered. It is only to be understood. The journey is never ending. There's always going to be growth, improvement, adversity. People need to take it, all in and do what's right, continue to grow and live in the moment.

Life stops when people stop dreaming. Hope ends, when people stop believing. Love ends, when people stop caring. Friendship ends, when people stop sharing.Be thankful for, what people have; they will end up having more. If we concentrate on, what we don't have, we will never, ever have enough. We don't realize, what we have got, until it's gone because we just thought, we would never lose it.Truth is simple, but the moment we try to explain, it becomes difficult.

Confidence is our best accessory, never leave home without it; it may not bring success but gives the power to face challenges.There will always be someone willing to hurt, put down, gossip, belittle accomplishments & judge one's soul. It is a fact that we all must face. However, if we realize that God is a best friend that stands beside us when others throw stones, we will never be afraid, never feel worthless & never feel alone. All truths are easy to understand, once they are discovered; the point is to discover them.

Caring about others, running the risk of feeling, & leaving an impact on people, brings happiness. The closest thing to being cared for is to care for someone else. Caring is a gift, that no one can buy. It's made up of love that roots in the hearts & creates memories, not just for a while but for a lifetime.If people want to be happy, do not dwell in the past, do not worry about the future, focus on living fully in the present. We all have the power to shape our day and life, so no matter what is happening in our lives, we can make the decision to be happy & enjoy every moment. Remember that setbacks are only challenges in disguise. Look at them, as lessons, don't waste time beating up. Just get back on track & focus on what we want. It's up to people,and they will do it. The comeback is always greater than the setback

Life is a compromise between feelings&reality. Many a time, we have to quit feelings & accept the reality. When it is obvious that goals cannot be reached, don't adjust the goals, adjust the action steps.Attitude is a choice.

Happiness is a choice. Optimism is a choice. Kindness is a choice. Giving is a choice. Respect is a choice. Whatever choice we make, Makes*Us*. Choose wisely.We all have the power to shape our day & life, so no matter what is happening in our lives we can make the decision to be happy & enjoy every moment.The main difference between attitude & ego is that; the attitude makes people different from others: while ego makes people alone from others. Apologizing does not always mean that the person is wrong& the other person is right. It just means, that they value relationship more than there ego.

Sip coffee nice & slow. No one ever knows, when it's time to go, there'll be no time to enjoy the glow, so sip coffee nice and slow. Life is too short but feels pretty long, there's too much to do, so much going wrong, and most of the time people struggle to be strong. Some friends stay, others go away, loved ones are cherished, but not all will stay, kids will grow up and fly away, there's really no saying, how things will go, sosip coffee nice and slow. In the end it's really, all about understanding love, for this world and in the stars above.

Appreciate and value,which truly cares, smile and breathe and let worries go, so, just sip the coffee nice and slow.Let's smile at the little things in life that put balm in our hearts. And yet, we must continue to enjoy serenely the time that remains. Let's try to eliminate the after I do it. I will say, afterI will think about it, after we leave everything for later, as if after was ours. Because what we do not understand is that: after, the coffee cools after, priorities change. After, the charm is broken, after, health passes. after, the children grow up after, the parents get older, after, the promises are forgotten, after, the day becomes the night, after, life ends, and after that it's often too late .so ... Leave nothing for later, because always waiting for later, can lose the best moments, the best experiences, the best friends, the best family. The day is today ... The moment is now

Positive thinking, may not guarantee success, but negative thinking definitelyguarantees failure. So, we should always have a positive attitude, keep face always toward the sunshine & shadows will fall behind. More information is always better than less. When people know the reason, things are happening, even if it's bad news, they can adjust their expectations & react accordingly. Keeping people in the dark, only serves to stir negative emotions. We must adjust to changing times & still hold to unchanging principles.

Hardly the day started and ... It is already six o'clock in the evening. Barely arrived on Monday and it's already Friday.... And the month is already over. ... And the year is almost up. ... And already 40, 50, 60 or 70 years of our lives have passed. ... And we realize that we lost our parents, friends.And we realize that it is too late to go back.so ... Let'stry; however, to take full advantage of the time, we have left.Let's not stop looking for activities that we like .Let's put color in our greyness.

We are no longer at the age, where we can afford to postpone until tomorrow, what needs to be done right away. Learn to enjoy every minute of life. Be happy now.Don't wait for something, outside of oneself to make a person happy in the future. Think how really precious is the time to spend, whether it's at work or with family. Every minute, should be enjoyed & savored.Know life is worth the struggle,when look back on what is lost, & realize what we have now, is way better than before.People never know, what's around the corner. It could be everything or nothing. Keep putting one foot, in front of the other, and then one day look back & they will release they have climbed a mountain. A river cuts through rock not because of its power but its persistence.

When the past gets its, teeth into our daily life, it may get to grip with an astringent reality & adjust our timeline. By recognizing ourselves in light of our history, we become aware of what we are. Don't live the same day over & over again & call that a life. Life is about evolving mentally, spiritually, & emotionally.

Don't turn face away, once seen by people, they can no longer act like they don't know. Open eyes to the truth. It's all around people. Don't deny what the eyes to soul have revealed to you.Now that people know, they cannotfeign ignorance. Now that they are aware of the problem, they cannot pretend that they don't care. To be concerned is to be human. To act is to care. Walking with the time is not necessary, but always walks with truth. One day automatically time will walk as per you

Life's too precious, so have fun, treasure the memories, say what one want's to, do what one want, have no regrets & remember everything happens for a reason.

When life goes wrong, don'twaste time, looking back to what onehas lost.For the road of life, was never meant to be traveled backwards just move on, as things always happen for a reason. Never try to test good people. Because, good people are like mercury. When people hit them, they will not break, but they just slip away from your life silently. We really don't find too many good people. If we really have some, around us. Keep them & be one such person for others.

We're so busy watching out for what's just ahead of us that we don't take time to enjoy where we are. Don't hurry through life. Don't worry through life. Life is not just to run. It's also to have some fun.The best will never be good enough, to the ones constantly searching for flaws. But for people to be the best, they need to ignore the flaws& do what is the best.Like a lotus flower, we too have the ability to rise from mud, bloom out of the darkness & radiate into the world.

The most beautiful things in life are not things. They're people & places and memories & pictures. They're feelings & moments & smiles & laughter. The more praise and celebrate our life, the more there is in life to celebrate.If weexamine a butterfly, according to the laws of aerodynamics, it shouldn't be able to fly. But the butterfly doesn't know that, so it flies. So, forget rule books. Do the best.People can have everything they want; if they can put heart & soul into everything.

Thoughts & actions not only influence the mood, but the moods of all cross paths with. Think lovingly. Do lovingly. Try to be a messenger of love than hatred.A beautiful life is just an imagination, but real life is more beautifulthan imagination. So, enjoy each & every moment of life.The pessimist sees difficulty in every opportunity. The optimist sees opportunity in every difficulty. We may encounter many defeats but we must not be defeated.

Motivation is like a food for the brain. People cannot get enough in one sitting. It needs continuous & regular refills. There is never an end to start something good, ☐ make a start and get a perfect end.

People are allborn with selfish desires, so they can all relate to those feelings in others. But kindness is something, made individually by each person. So it's easy to misunderstand, when others are trying to be kind. A big-hearted soul does not sentence others on the basis of a single act, but appreciates others through understanding their entire journey.

Never let one head hang down. Never give up & sit down and grieve. Find another way. And don't pray, when it rains if one never pray's when the sun shines.The difference between what we do and are capable of doing would suffice to solve most of the world's problems. If we want to be successful, it's just this simple. Know what we are doing. Love, what we are doing & believe in, what we are doing. We normally say time changes & so do people, but the fact is, neither time changes nor people. Onlything, which changes with the time, are priorities. All of dreams can come true, if we have the courage to pursue them. There is no going back in life, what has happened, has happened & the only way, is the way forward.

Life is a series of natural and spontaneous changes. Don't resist them; that only creates sorrow. Let reality be reality. Let things flow naturally forward, in whatever, way they like. Highest form of maturity, is the making of constant changes, while walking the righteous & virtuous path, with courage, wisdom & conviction

Don't be afraid to start over. Don't be afraid to listen to intuitions, even if, it appears to be leading away, from what's safe & comfortable. Trust the unknown, holds to next chapter. Don't try to comprehend with mind. People mindis very limited. Use intuition. Knowledge gained through experience is far superior and many times more useful than bookish knowledge. Information is not knowledge. The only source of knowledge is experience. People need experience, to gain wisdom.Wake up every morning, with the idea that something wonderful is possible today. Smiling is a healing energy.Always find a reason to smile. It may not add years to life but will surely add life to one's years.A consistent positive attitude is the cheapest 'fountain of youth. One got to dance, like there's nobody watching, love like one will never be hurt, sing like there's nobody listening, & live like it's heaven on earth.Life is very short to argue and fight. Count blessings, valuable friends& move on with head held high & a smile for everyone.

Whatever heart is telling today, act on it. Don't wait, until tomorrow to start doing, what's necessary for the journey. This chapter of life is called. Take initiative.   Make smart decisions & move forward with grace & humility.People should always believe they are not the same person they used to be & there are some improvements,which is a fact worth celebrating. Start now; don't wait another second to live magical life, one has dreamed of.A life lived, without risks, pretty much wasn't worth living.Life rewarded courage, even when that first step was taken neck-deep in fear. Maybe, sometimes it's riskier not to take a risk. Sometimes all you're guaranteeing is that things will stay the same!

If people have a dream, don't just sit there. Gather courage to believe that they can succeed & leave no stone unturned to make it, a reality. The will to win. The desire to succeed. The urge to reach full potential, these are the keys that will unlock the door to personal excellence.One can't decide the length of life, but can very well control how they want to live it. They can't control the weather, butcan control mood. Can't change their look, but can very well smile to make it better.

People can't control others, but can very well control themselves .They can't foresee tomorrow, but can very well utilize today wisely. They can't win everything, but can very well try very best to achieve that. Face the daily life, positively & be always happy, today &every day. Everybody isn't friend. Just because they hang around you & laugh with you, doesn't mean they are true friends. People pretend well. At the end of the day, real situations expose fake people, so we'd always pay attention.A fake person will make a mistake & act like it never happened. A real person will make a mistake, admit it & apologize regardless of the outcome!When find no solution to a problem, it's probably, not a problem to be solved, but a truth to be accepted. If we can, accept the truth & live with it, our heart will be at peace, for whatever our we are going through. It might be preparation, for what to come. A hard or difficult time, is humbling, soone may enjoy the most out of the prosperous season to come.We all have the power to shape our day & life, so no matter, what is happening in our lives, we can make decision to be happy & enjoy every moment.

When situations bring one downon knees, remember, that they are in a perfect position to pray &their prayer will make one standon feet again with greater strength. Prayer is the song of the heart. It reaches the ear of god, even if it is mingled with the cry & tumult of a thousand men.Human greatness does not lie in wealth or power, but in character & goodness. People are just people & all people have faults & shortcomings, but all of us are born with a basic goodness. Greatness is not found, in possessions, power, position, or prestige. It is discovered in goodness, humility, service, character.

The happiness of lifedepends upon the quality of thoughts, therefore, guard accordingly, & take care that one entertains, no notions unsuitable to virtue & reasonable nature. We are shaped by our thoughts; we become what we think. When the mind is pure, joy follows like a shadow that never leaves.

Good behavior can cover lack of good looks; but, good looks can never cover lack of good behavior. We change other people's behavior, by changing our own!The pain is temporary. It may last a minute, an hour, a day, or a year, but eventually it subsides. And when it does, something else takes its place, and that thing might, be called a greater space for happiness. If we quit however, it will last forever. Each time we overcome pain, we grow.

Life is full of challenges, but these challenges are only given to people because god knows that their   faith is strong enough to get them through. The challenges,they are experiencing right now are going to give them a victorious feeling very soon. Just keep moving towards breakthrough.

If people experience any emotion like frustration, hesitation or anger, while planning a dream life, means,they need to clear some mental blocks. Don't let mental blocks control one .Set oneself free. Confront fear& turn the mental blocks into building blocks of success.The optimist pleasantly ponders how high his kite will fly; the pessimist woefully wonders how soon his kite will fall. A pessimist sees difficulty, in every opportunity; an optimist sees opportunity in every difficulty.Always isan optimist. If people spend life, concentrating on, what everyone else thought of them,they would forget, who they really were? What if face showed world turned out to be a mask.With nothing beneath it. Everyone seems to have a clear idea of how other people should lead their lives, but none about his or her own.

If people want a better and happier life, they need to learn about forgiveness. Practice forgiveness, & do it, to release from holding those negative feelings,in heart, mind & soul.Darkness cannot drive out darkness; only light can do that. Hate cannot drive out hate; only love can do that.Even if one cannotchange all the people, around him,they can change the people he chooses to be around. Life is too short to waste time on people who don't respect,appreciate, & value. Spend life with people, who make one smile, laugh, & feel loved. Until let go of all the toxic people in life, one will never be able to grow into fullest potential. Let them go, so that one can grow.

Life is too short, to spend our precious time, trying to convince a person who wants to live in gloom & doom otherwise. Give lifting, that person your best shot, but don't hang around long enough for his or her bad attitude to pull you down. Instead, surround with optimistic people. Pessimism never won any battle.If we desire to blossom like a rose in the garden, then we must learn the art, of adjusting with the thorns. Remember, difficulties will make you shine. Do not let difficulties fill with anxiety. After all, it is only in the darkest night that stars shine more brightly.

Experiences are like Waves

Experiences are like waves. They come to us on the shore of life; drag the sand from beneath our feet. But each wave makes us, stand on a new base. Life is a succession of lessons, which must be lived to be understood.Everybody isn't our friend. Just because they hang around & laugh with us doesn't mean, they are our friends. People pretend well. At the end of day, real situations expose fake people, so pay attention. A fake person will make a mistake and act like it never happened. A real person will make a mistake, admit it & apologize regardless of the outcome!

Life is too short to spend your precious time trying to convince a person, who wants to live in gloom & doom otherwise. Give lifting that person, but don't hang around, long enough for his or her bad attitude to pull down. Instead, surround with optimistic people. Optimism is the faith that leads to achievement. Nothing can be done without hope & confidence.

It is not always possible to do away with negative thinking, but with persistence &practice, one can gain mastery over them, so that they do not take the upper hand. Our thoughts carry us, whereverwe want to go. Weak thoughts don't have the energy to carry us far! We cannot change circumstances, seasons, or wind, but we can change toprotect & take benefits of the said changes. Wise change is necessary for sustainable growth. Nothing can be changed by changing, the face but everything can be changed by facing the change! Always move ahead, with confidence & covert changed circumstances to benefits.

We are all born with a certain degree of power. The key to success is discovering this innate power & using it daily to deal with whatever challenges come our way. Our ability to handle life's challenges is a measure of our strength of character. Smile is our logo; our personality is our business card. How we leave others, feeling after having an experience with us becomes our trademark.When life gives a hundred reasons to break down & cry, show life that we have a million reasons to smile &laugh. All blame is a waste of time. No matter, how much fault we find with another, & regardless of how much,we blame him, it will not change us .The only thing blame does, is to keep the focus off, when we are looking for reasons to explain unhappiness or frustration. Take accountability... Blame is the water, in which many dreams & relationships drown.

Self-Control and Concentration

Self- control is strength. Calmness is mastery. We have to get to a point, where our mood doesn't shift, based on the insignificant actions of someone else. Never respond to an angry person, with a fiery comeback, even if he deserves. When we open our eyes in the morning, sit for a moment & appreciate the gift of a new day, create a peaceful thought & enjoy some moments of silence, throughout the whole day. Be thankful for what we have; we'll end up having more. If we concentrate on, what we don't have, we will never, ever have enough. One who understands difference between more' & 'enough is the happiest person in the world.

Champions aren't made in schools/ colleges or gyms. Champions are made from something, they have deep inside them—a desire, a dream, a vision. They have to have the skill & will, but the will must be stronger than the skill. There are many players in the game, but only champions have strong self-belief.Mistakes matter. How we recover, from them matters even more. The best way to handle a mistake is to learn from the mistake. Then we'll not repeat it nor ever be paralyzed by the fear of making another mistake. Anyone, who has never made a mistake, has never tried anything new.

Happiness is not so much in having as sharing. We make a living, by what we get, but we make a life, by what we give! Thousands of candles can be lighted, from a single candle, & the life of candle will not be shortened. Happiness never decreases by being shared.

Summary

The confidence is reflection of positive power of human personality. People can grow through their faith and values of life. The empowerment and confidence of believing in oneself, can build the ethical aspects of human life. The creative ability of people can generally be designed by the power ofbeing connected to the ethics of performing their work and duties in in systematic way.

Life is not just about the good things or not just about the bad things. It is both. It all depends where we focus our attention. Good things come to those who believe, better things come to those who are patient, & the best things come to those who don't give up. No one is without troubles, personal hardships & genuine challenges. Challenges, failures, defeats & ultimately, progress, are what make our life worthwhile.